Basics of Business Management series

Booklet 4

Human Resources Management

(It is integral to your job)

CW00498508

A.S. Srinivasan

Clever Fox
PUBLISHING

Chennai • Bangalore

CLEVER FOX PUBLISHING
Chennai, India

Published by CLEVER FOX PUBLISHING 2023
Copyright © A.S.Srinivasan 2023

All Rights Reserved.
ISBN: 978-93-56482-16-6

Human Resources Management

*Based on my booklet **A Concise Guide to Basics of Business Management**, I thought it would be appropriate to outline major concepts and practices under each functional area as well as business strategy in greater detail in the form of booklets. Thus, along with the **Concise Guide**, these booklets will give a more detailed coverage of these concepts in the field of business management.*

Of course, each concept in itself has been covered and discussed in great detail by many scholars and there are innumerable books on each of them. No one small booklet like this one, can claim to do justice to all of them in a few pages. This is just a distilled and brief outline of them which again is intended to give an overview of these classic concepts so that the reader becomes familiar with them.

*I have reproduced my Introduction, References and Afterword from my booklet **A Concise Guide to Basics of Business Management** since these booklets will also serve the same purpose to the same audience and are from the same sources. Nothing stated here are original and are based entirely on the materials mentioned in Introduction. I was fortunate to have had the opportunity to study them. Where necessary, I have taken the liberty of using them to preserve their meaning. The errors and misunderstandings are purely result of my limited knowledge and exposure.*

***Booklet 4** in this series is on **Human Resources Management**. In the classical sense, managing is primarily managing people and as such, Human Resources Management forms the core in any study of basics of management.*

Topics covered in this booklet are: Understanding human behaviour at individual, group and organisational levels, Motivating people,

Leadership essentials, Managing performance and development and Managing change etc.

I only hope that an in-depth understanding of the topics covered in this booklet leads you to become a complete manager and onwards to a great leader.

A.S. Srinivasan   **October, 2022**

A Concise Guide to Basics of Business Management

Introduction

This booklet will be of use to all those who are interested in the field of Business Management. If you are a practising manager or an entrepreneur, this could serve as a refresher. If you have recently taken up a managerial position, this will be a useful reference book for you to look at some of the concepts mentioned here. If you are a student or a person interested to know the basics of management, this will serve the purpose of a guidebook.

This booklet is brief but comprehensive, outlining all the major management concepts and practices in all functional areas. As a manager in today's highly competitive and dynamic business environment, you need to

1. *Develop the capability to look at your organisation's business holistically*

2. *Become familiar with major concepts and practices in all functional areas of management*

3. *Understand the integrated nature of your business, the interconnectedness of various functions and the impact of your individual and departmental decisions and actions on the total operations of the company and*

4. *Have the urge to develop yourself further to meet the challenges of today and tomorrow*

Hopefully, this booklet will help you embark on this journey of life-long learning.

I have primarily relied on various management books by leading authors in compiling all the concepts presented here which I gratefully acknowledge. I claim no originality or ownership of these ideas. I have gathered these over the years I was serving in academics. I have appended a list of primary references and have mentioned the names of original thinkers and writers in my text at appropriate places. There are many more that are in public domain which I have used in presenting these contents.

All these classic concepts have been mentioned very briefly and need further study for greater understanding. This is in no way a textbook. It is just a window to the field of management. This booklet will have served its purpose if it arouses your curiosity to know more on any topic or concept you are interested in. I look forward to receiving your comments and feedback.

Welcome to a short journey through this fascinating field of management!

A.S. Srinivasan   **October, 2022**

Human Resources Management

In the preceding booklet 3 on "Marketing Management", we had covered major concepts and practices in an important functional area of management- Marketing. We now move on to arguably the most important aspect of management- managing people.

We will look at the major components of Human Resources Management under the following broad sections:

1. Understanding human behaviour at individual, group and organisational levels

2. Motivating people, the key to success

3. Leadership essentials

4. Managing performance and development

5. Managing change

As we know, management is primarily an activity consisting of working with other people and as a manager, your main task is to integrate performance of people reporting to you and empower them for greater performance. Hence, any person desirous of becoming a "manager" in the true sense of the word, that too a successful one, has to understand the basic principles and practices in managing people and the art of managing people. It is an art in the sense that it cannot be reduced to mere numbers based purely on rational decision making. Also, it is a two-way process and involves human beings who are also driven by emotion as much as by reason and can react in unexpected ways. Further, in managing people ethical and moral considerations are involved. Other factors to be considered in managing people are:

- Output of people is not fixed. It depends on the level of motivation, a basic challenge in managing people.

- Since human beings are inherently sociable, relationships-both positive and negative are important. When more and more people are involved, these become complex and affect both the working atmosphere and output.

- Unlike other resources, human resources do not get consumed. By equipping people with newer skills and greater capabilities, you can enhance their output.

Thus, managing people is complex and is different from managing other resources and one needs to tread with caution and sensitivity when dealing with people.

Hence, it would be appropriate for us to start with the topic of understanding human behaviour as the first step in managing people. We will then follow up with managing motivation and basic requirements for successful leadership. Subsequently, we will cover the topics of managing performance and development of people and finally look at how to manage change since everything keeps changing and we should be able to handle challenges in a change situation.

We need to understand ourselves as well as others as the first step in managing people. We will look at human behaviour at three levels:

- Individual
- interpersonal
- Organisational (Groups)

1. Understanding individual behaviour:

Our behaviour as individuals depends on several factors - some are in-born, some based on our childhood and near environment and others develop at different stages of our life cycle as we grow and interact with outside world of people in our neighbourhood, community, educational institutions, workplace, society etc. Some aspects of our behaviour keep changing over time but many remain with us until death.

1.1 Individual behaviour:

We need to look at the following factors in understanding individual behaviour:

i. Biological characteristics like age, gender, physical features etc.

ii. Personality and cognitive factors: Personality refers to the individual's pattern of thinking, feeling and behaving. Cognition is the process involved in knowing based on individual's perception and judgement. It includes both conscious and unconscious processes by which we gather knowledge consisting of perceiving, recognising, conceiving and reasoning. These depend on our heredity- family, immediate background and situation.

Personality also includes our own perception of locus of control. This is the degree to which we believe that we are in control over outcomes of events in our lives or they depend on other people or fate.

iii. Values: A person's value system consists of standards and self-discipline set by the individual based on his/her own common sense and understanding of what moral and discipline standards are. Thus, it varies from person to person based on their own standards. These are classified into two categories:

• Terminal values are those which we think are the most important or the most desirable ones which we would like to achieve during our lifetime. They include self-respect, recognition, harmony, leading a prosperous and happy life, professional excellence etc.

- Instrumental values are those which help in achieving our terminal values. Examples are: Being honest and hardworking, sincere, ethical, ambitious etc.

iv. Abilities: These include our skills, capabilities, talent, competence etc consisting of our physical, intellectual and learning abilities. Some of them are acquired and some are inborn. Aptitude refers to those abilities for which we have a natural inclination.

v. Attitude: This reflects our feelings, positions etc with reference to a person, activity or object. Attitude could be positive, negative or neutral.

vi. Perception: This is the way we understand and interpret things from what we see, hear and learn.

vii. Emotions: These are our responses or feelings developed towards someone or something based on our relationships, circumstances and moods.

1.2 Personality type and cognitive or learning style:

These contribute to our preference for working and behaving in certain ways like

- How we relate to others
- How we communicate
- How we learn
- How we solve problems etc

Nowadays, sophisticated tools have been developed and used in determining our personality types. The two major inventories used in deciding our personality type are:

- MBTI personality types
- KAI inventory

Further developments are going on in other tools like "The Big Five" personality types, desirable and undesirable traits of each of them etc.

i. MBTI (Myers Briggs Type Indicator):This inventory administers a structured questionnaire and the answers are tabulated and grouped to arrive at which your dominant personality type is. The groupings are:

- How we relate to others and the world: Extroversion (E) Vs. Introversion (I)
- The way we gather information: Sensing (S) Vs. Intuition (N)
- The way we make decisions: Thinking (T) Vs. Feeling (F)
- The way we choose priorities Judging (J) Vs. Perceiving (P)

These classifications indicate our preferences in these groups and the various types of personalities are combinations of these factors such as ENFJ or ISTP etc.

ii. KAI inventory: This inventory (Kirton Adaptor/Innovator inventory) helps in understanding whether one adapts to existing things or the person is inclined to do things differently.

iii. Learning style inventory (LSI): This inventory classifies people's dominant learning styles into

- Activist
- Reflector
- Theorist
- Pragmatist

iv. The Big Five personality traits: The big five traits that are measured through various methods in the recent years are:

- Openness to experience
- Conscientiousness
- Extroversion
- Agreeableness
- Neuroticism

A word of caution is in order here. While these inventories indicate one's inclinations and preferences, there are often overlaps and strict box-fitting people on this basis alone is not desirable. Also, they are not comprehensive in the sense that there are other factors that influence a person's individual behaviour. They primarily help us understand how group and organisational behaviour are influenced and affected by these factors in a group/organisational setting.

1.3 Understanding individual behaviour:

Having seen factors that determine an individual's behaviour, we will now move on to analyse how we can understand a person's behaviour. Primarily, two areas are to be considered as follows:

- We need to appreciate the point of view of the person involved
- We also need to see how his/her behaviour is affected by the pressures, constraints and conventions that are dictated by the society.

i. Rational individualist view of behaviour:

This view states that an individual is in charge of his/her behaviour. Every person has his/her own mental models to "construct" events. These are based on the individual's experience. Hence, we need to understand the person's "repertory grid" to make sense of behaviour. This is based on the technique developed by Mr. George Kelly. This is a way of conducting an interview in a highly structured manner used to measure the personality of the individual.

ii. Other inputs that go into behaviour are the values and goals of the individual.

Values that dictate behaviour may be grouped into:

• Individual values

• Professional values

• Group/team values

• Organisational values etc.

We will be seeing more of these under ethics.

We should understand that a person's goals also dictate behaviour.

iii. Another point of view of behaviour is that all behaviour is result of social pressure the individual undergoes. According to this view, people behave as per the "rules of the game" based on the role he/she plays. Thus, an individual's behaviour at home and in the organisational setting may be quite different.

iv. Whichever view we may hold, the pitfall to be avoided in understanding another person's behaviour is that we should not judge it from our point of view which is based on our own goals and values.

2. Interpersonal behaviour:

Generally, we can use the theory of Transactional Analysis (TA) developed by Canadian-born psychiatrist Eric Berne in late 1950s. Though originally developed for psychotherapy, it finds application in understanding all interpersonal transactions. It explains how an individual's behaviour changes based equally on the behaviour of the other person with whom he/she is interacting. The concept of TA was made popular by American psychiatrist Dr Thomas A Harris in his best seller book titled "I am OK - You are OK", published in 1967.

i. According to Dr. Berne, there are four psychological positions a person can hold. They are:

*   "I am OK and you are OK": This is the healthiest position a person can take, feeling good about one's own self and also the same about the other person.

*   "I am OK and you are not OK": Here, the person feels he is good, but the other person is not.

*   "I am not OK and you are OK": In this, the individual sees himself/herself as a weak partner and the other person as better or superior.

*   "I am not OK and you are not OK": This is the least healthy position to take since the person feels both he/she and the others are all bad.

ii. Applying TA to understand interpersonal relationships: As per Dr. Berne, based on TA, we can see that each individual is a complex and shifting combination of three distinct sub-personalities as follows:

*   Parent
*   Adult
*   Child

We can further classify these states into:

- Parent: Critical parent or nurturing patient
- Adult: Rational, objective, practical
- Child: Free child, Adapted child or Rebellious child
  Free child: Natural, uninhibited and spontaneous
  Adapted child: Wants recognition and rewards. Behaviour changes accordingly to compliant or sulking
  Rebellious child: Defiant, hostile

iii. We can see the interrelationship patterns when each of the parties takes one or the other of the positions mentioned above:

- When both are in "Adult" state: I am OK and you are OK
- When one is in "Parent" and the other in "Child" state: I am OK and you are not OK
- When both are in "Child" state: I am not OK and you are not OK

3. Group Behaviour: (Organisational Behaviour - OB):

We will now move on from individual and interpersonal to group behaviour. Since groups and teams are the basic units of organisations, this is called as Organisational behaviour or OB. This topic can be studied in conjunction with other topics covered in my Booklet 2 on Managing in Organisations which dealt with basics of Organisations, their Culture, Structure, Systems and Processes etc.

3.1 Groups and teams:

i. Why people work in groups: As we know, working with

other people is a group activity. Often, people work together for the following reasons:

- They share and participate in a common activity towards achieving a particular objective
- This activity establishes a common identity
- Working in groups satisfies social needs of people

ii. Groups and teams: These two terms are mostly used interchangeably, though there are certain differences which make teams stand apart as listed below:

- In a team, each member has a specific role to play. An appropriate example is different roles played by each member in games like cricket, football etc
- They work towards a common task or a goal
- The work of members are interdependent. This is called teamwork

In a group, these are not strictly applicable. It could just be an assembly of people. However, we will use both terms interchangeably for our discussions.

While organisations depend on groups and teams to achieve their objectives, there are times when an individual can best work alone, like in cases where the tasks are simple and clear and speed of execution is of essence. This also helps where an individual has certain innovative ideas which he/she could try out by oneself.

3.2   Improving the effectiveness of groups:

Making teams and groups more effective has always been a major challenge in managing people. We can classify the factors that affect group effectiveness into two categories: contextual and internal factors.

i. Contextual factors: These are given factors decided by the management and often fall outside the control of group members: They include:

    •   Size: It is said that an ideal size of a group should not exceed 10 or 12. This will ensure enough diversity and at the same time, lead to cohesion.

    •   Composition: While the task will dictate the group composition, if all the members have the same disposition viz. if the group is homogenous, there will be less conflict. But this will not be suitable for complex or creative tasks. On the other hand, if it is too diverse and individual thinking of members are very divergent, it may foster creativity. But at the same time, there are chances of greater conflict among members resulting in chaos and disorder.

    •   Task assigned: The task should be seen to be important in the achievement of company's objectives by the group members. It must also be realistic. These will enthuse the members giving meaning to their collective efforts.

    •   Support and resources: Management must provide adequate resources and extend necessary support.

    •   Recognition: Following this, the group members will be motivated to perform their best if their work is recognised by other members outside the group and the management of the organisation.

ii. Internal factors: Basically, there are two major factors that are internal to the group which affect the group effectiveness. They are:

    Leadership: We will be discussing the topic of leadership in greater detail later and confine ourselves to a group setting here. It goes without saying that leader's style of functioning is of critical importance. He/she has to direct as well as delegate based on the nature of the problem and task to be performed. Some of the major areas to be considered are:

- His/her primary responsibility is to assign tasks and responsibilities suitably to individual members based on a systematic and rational problem-solving approach

- At the same time, the leader has to create a conducive climate for peak performance by maintaining the morale and harmony of group members. Thus, it is achieving an optimal balance of "mind and heart", "rational and emotional".

Interaction among group members: Equally important are the interactions among group members. There has to be a spirit of camaraderie and mutual respect between them. Relationships within the group have to be free, cordial and one of mutual help with free flow of information.

3.3 Problems faced in groups:

Various problems people come across while working in groups may be classified into the following:

i. Hidden agendas: Here, members may have their own individual agendas or plans without revealing them. Because of these, the group becomes dysfunctional and will not be able to meet its objectives

ii. Group anxiety: When people work in groups, some of them may feel anxious about themselves, their inability to participate in group discussions, activities etc. A way out is for the leader to counsel the member concerned and put him/her at ease while in the group

iii. Group think: This arises when all members agree on a decision without critically analysing the pros and cons and the consequences of it. People do this mainly to conform and all the more, if it is a directive from the leader. There are several real-life examples of group think where major decisions were taken without any dissent that led to disastrous consequences. The solution may lie in a rigorous, rational problem-solving approach and an openness among members as well as with the leader.

3.4 Major causes for problems in group working:

Primarily, these problems are a result of unhelpful and non-cooperative attitudes and behaviour of members. Some of them are:

i. Self-orientation: Individual members may withdraw from, dominate or show-off in group discussions. They may also do this for belittling the contribution of another person to "score points".

ii. Seniority: Often, groups consist of people at different levels. Sometimes, the boss may also be a member. This perceived hierarchical dichotomy affects group work. Some of the group members may not participate in the presence of seniors or persons whom they think, have superior knowledge.

iii. Inequalities: Some of the members may have greater access to information. They may have greater skills and knowledge and may also have higher commitment to the task. These persons tend to dominate group discussions and activities at the exclusion of other members.

4. Teams:

4.1 Team roles:

As we saw earlier, in teams each member has a specific role to play. While these roles are assigned based on the member's technical or other expertise, many qualitative personality traits also determine how well the member plays the role assigned. Prof. R. M. Belbin of England has developed a framework for the various roles that are to be played in a team setting and the requisite qualities so that the team as a whole succeeds. The various roles (as patented by him) are given below. The names are self-explanatory.

- Implementor
- Co-ordinator
- Shaper
- Plant
- Resource investigator
- Monitor/Evaluator
- Team worker
- Completer/Finisher

We can see that the qualities required to perform each of these roles are different. Companies will do well to think through the process of team formation by choosing persons who have the natural inclination and traits so that they automatically assume their roles in a team setting.

It is often said that you do not need a team of the most talented persons to win. In fact, such a team may not perform as well as a team consisting of members with traits needed to perform the above-mentioned roles.

4.2 Stages in team functioning process:

Broadly, teams go through four or five distinct stages before they become a high-performance team on an ongoing project or wound up on completion of the specific objective for which they are formed. Following are the stages:

- Forming: At this first stage, the team is formed and starts functioning as a working group. Socialisation among team members takes place whereby they get to know each other.

- Storming: During this stage, individual members may start asserting themselves and try to assume the role of the leader. Confusion prevails on team goals and individual responsibilities.

- Norming: These conflicts and confusion get resolved at this stage. Clarity emerges in terms of team goals, sub-goals, leadership and individual roles. All team members get committed to team goals.

- Performing: Next stage is where the group effectiveness peaks up and individual members and team as a whole, are well on their way to achieve the goals.

- Adjourning: As mentioned earlier, teams working on long term goals, continue to perform and become highly effective. Team members adjust their roles to meet the emerging challenges. Teams formed for specific goals are disbanded after these have been achieved.

4.3 Basic factors enabling high team performance:

As the case in any situation where people work together, following factors help minimise conflicts and maximise team performance:

- Establishing clear and specific goals to be achieved by the team as a whole, with resources and time frame in place.

- Clarifying and assigning individual sub-goals and tasks to each member.

- Developing mutual trust, respect and team spirit among all members.

These enable teams to become high-performance teams.

5. Managing conflicts:

5.1 Conflicts:

As we know, whenever people work together a social dynamic is created. It is but natural that conflicts and disagreements arise in course of group activities in an organisational setting. Hence, managing conflicts and disagreements before they become dysfunctional is one of the major aspects of managing people.

It is a fact that some people have the natural ability in developing good relationships with others. You need to develop this ability and following aspects of managing conflicts may be of help to you in this regard. Power is the potential to influence others and we will explore this also along with other aspects.

5.2 Sources and types of conflicts:

- Conflicts can be overt or covert. Overt conflicts are in the open and are apparent. While often they are disagreements expressed openly, sometimes they may even lead to violent physical fights! On the other hand, covert conflicts are difficult to see and diagnose since either or both parties may have hidden reasons for their positions.

- Conflicts can be constructive or destructive. When resolved, constructive conflicts will lead to a win-win

20

situation where both parties are satisfied and work together. Destructive conflicts will lead to a win-lose situation where either of the parties may not fully co-operate with the resolution or agreement reached.

- Covert conflicts often arise due to misunderstanding of the issues involved or fear of consequences. Either of the parties may feel that they have not been consulted in the decisions taken. Also, one of them may harbour questions on whether the other party is the legitimate authority.

- When one of the parties is highly assertive, it could force a solution. The other party may avoid implementing the solution or not co-operate. When both parties express their positions clearly, understand and appreciate each other's position, higher co-operation will result.

- Apart from rational analysis, conflicts may arise due to differences in each other in their interests, feelings, emotions, values, beliefs etc.

5.3 Power:

i. Power and authority: As we saw a while ago, power is the capacity of a person or a group of people to influence other people. While this is applicable in all cases of Politics, Society, Community, Family etc, we look at power specifically with reference to business organisations here. Naturally, a person or a group has to have the power to ensure that others in the organisation follow the rules and regulations in achievement of goals of the organisation as a whole or sub-units. When this power is formally given to them, it becomes authority bestowed on them because of their position or role.

ii. Sources of power: Apart from authority or position-based power, the other sources of power are:

- Control of resources: Resources are required to carry out the tasks assigned and naturally whoever controls the resources, wields power to that extent. It could be the finance manager controlling finances or HR manager controlling the extent of people assigned to the task or the marketing manager who decides the advertising and promotional spend.

- Expertise: Power comes to people who have the expertise and special knowledge in a particular area. It could be a technical expert, scientist, economist etc.

- Social connections: There are several examples where the relatives of promoters or senior managers exercise a lot of power. Some may turn out to be good for the organisation and some may not.

- Personal characteristics and excellence in developing interpersonal relations: These are important factors especially in the exercise of informal power. Often these people emerge and/or sought after as informal leaders and influencers.

- These sources are not mutually exclusive and are inter-related in the emergence of power centre/centres in the organisation.

5.4 Resolving conflicts:

As a manager, one of your primary responsibilities is to resolve unhealthy conflicts between individuals, intra-group members, between groups and also with outsiders like trade, labour union etc.

i. Options: When you are faced with interpersonal or inter-group conflicts, depending on the causes of conflict and situation, you can do one of the following:

- Non-intervention: Leave it to the people concerned to resolve their conflicts among themselves, by not intervening.

- Prevention: If you can foresee a potential conflict situation, you can prevent by taking early steps like counselling etc.

- Use power and/or facilitate resolution: If the situation develops further, your intervention will become necessary. In this case, you can exercise your power suitably. You can also facilitate resolution by making both parties discuss and overcome differences. In certain other cases, you may have to negotiate and try to arrive at a win-win situation.

ii. Some general principles useful in resolving conflicts:

- Establishing and clarifying common goals so that misunderstandings are eliminated.

- Improving the process of communication between members and groups.

- Resorting to "push" strategies like imposing a resolution by using your power.

- Using "pull" strategies like rewarding resolution and by engaging in negotiation

Ultimately, as a manager your aim should be to reach a win-win situation so that all concerned understand and implement the decisions taken for the betterment of everyone and achievement of goals set.

5.5 The science and art of negotiating:

While some people have the natural ability in negotiating successfully with persons whose position is different from theirs, there are certain guidelines that will help you negotiate effectively.

- First of all, you need to separate people from the problem by showing your genuine interest in resolving the issue without attributing it to people.

- You need to clarify on the objective criteria to be analysed in the conflict resolution

- You must ensure that people do not take hard positions by prioritising interests of all concerned.

- You can generate mutually acceptable alternatives in a spirit of "give and take" leading to a win-win resolution.

All these topics come under the broad area Group Behaviour or Human Behaviour in Organisations.

6. Understanding and managing motivation:

We all know that the primary factor that drives people to do their best is motivation. This is often explained by the simple equation: Performance = Ability X Motivation. Hence, if people are not motivated whatever abilities they may have, the result is zero performance.

Almost invariably, motivating one's subordinates and team members is the primary job of a manager since he/she is uniquely placed to shoulder this responsibility. Motivation is what makes people work hard and enthusiastically and persist in overcoming any problems that may arise. Motivation is what makes people commit to their job, organisation, their personal and organisational values, goals etc.

6.1 Theories of motivation:

While there are several theories on motivation, in reality

different combinations of them work in different situations. We will briefly see the highlights of each of them here.

i.   The Social Needs model: This is based on Prof. Elton Mayo's experiments in a telephone factory in the USA in 1933 and probably, the path breaker in the study of human relations and motivation. It challenged the classical approach based on Prof. Fredrick Taylor's theory which gave primacy to productivity as the aim of managers.

Prof. Elton Mayo postulated that being essentially social animals, human beings perform better when their social needs are met and when they work in groups. As we will see later, this is widely applied in all job designs and group assignments.

ii. Maslow's theory of Needs Hierarchy: This is the celebrated model of pyramid of human needs by Prof. Maslow. According to this model, human needs may be grouped into several steps of a ladder progressing from the lowest rung to higher rungs as follows:

•   Self-actualisation ...   Highest
•   Self esteem
•   Love/belonging
•   Safety
•   Physiological ... ...   Lowest

These terms are self-explanatory. Starting with basic needs of food, clothing and shelter at physiological level, once these needs are satisfied human needs go up progressively to next level of safety where one's personal safety becomes the concern. The next level is to look for love and sense of belonging in terms of family, group, community etc. Following this, individuals want to fulfil their self-esteem needs where they want to be recognised and respected by people around them. Once they are satisfied, they go beyond and work for a cause bigger than one's own needs and by continuing to work for its fulfilment, their self-actualisation needs are met.

While there is a lot of merit in this model, the main criticism is that these needs are not really in a hierarchical order. A person can work for self-esteem or self-actualisation even as his/her basic needs are yet to be fully met. We see this practically in our lives especially in modern times where needs keep multiplying (like big, bigger and bigger and better) and on one hand, people get stuck working in fulfilling them only and do not move up to the next level. On the other hand, there are people who work for self-actualisation goals even before meeting other needs.

iii.   Herzberg's two-factor theory: Another American psychologist Prof. Herzberg proposed the two-factor theory of motivation which is also widely recognised. He divides the motivational factors into two groups- Hygiene factors and Motivation factors.

Hygiene factors by themselves do not motivate people to perform their best, but their absence will lead to demotivation and dissatisfaction. Factors that come under this group include:

• Pay
• Job security
• Working conditions
• Interpersonal relations
• Supervision quality
• Company policies

Their absence leads to dissatisfied employees, employee turnover, absenteeism etc.

On the other hand, motivation factors consist of:

- The content and scope of work itself
- The level of responsibility assigned
- Recognition for job well done
- Scope for advancement and growth
- Sense of achievement and fulfilment on completing the job successfully

Only when these factors are present, a person is motivated to put forth his/her best efforts on the job assigned. We can see that these are becoming more and more important in the present industrial world, especially in the case of knowledge workers. It is almost universal now that basic hygiene factors have to be provided to retain people at all levels and these are taken for granted. It is the presence of motivation factors that leads to excellence in performance and "loyalty" to the organisation.

iv. Equity theory: This theory states that being social animals, human beings always tend to compare inputs given by them to their jobs with those of people they choose for comparison. Similarly, they judge outcomes on a comparable basis like pay, benefits, status, job satisfaction etc. If they find them similar, they feel motivated. If they perceive that what they get are lower than these people, they are dissatisfied.

In these cases, the judgment of equity is entirely that of the individual even when the organisation may feel that it has rewarded the person objectively. Thus, perception is as important as reality and we all know that this comparison is very real and is an important factor to be considered.

v.   Expectancy theory: Here three factors are considered: expectancy, instrumentality and valence which determine the level of motivation.

Expectancy: The individual sees the connect between his/her effort and performance (output). Higher the degree of connect, higher the motivation since the expectancy level is largely met.

Instrumentality: Here the person connects performance (output) with outcome (rewards), again higher the perceived connect, higher the motivation.

Valence: In this case, the person expects the reward (outcome) to match his /her desired reward. It is the attractiveness of the outcome or reward to the individual.

Thus, in the chain of Expectancy – Performance – Outcome, if the person perceives high degree of correlation, motivation level is high. This should help the manager in deciding the right job for the right person and match the reward expected for satisfactory performance.

vi.   Learned Needs theory: This theory propounded by Dr. David McClelland of the Harvard University, USA, is especially applicable in the case of motivating managerial people. He has listed three needs as strong motivators which are often learned during life experience of the manager. These are:

•   Need for achievement

•   Need for affiliation

•   Need for power

Need for achievement motivates people to accept responsibility since they like to set challenging goals and achieve them.

Persons with need for affiliation want to be accepted and act as a part of a group.

Need for power is a very strong motivating factor especially in the case of leaders who want to influence behaviour of others and lead them.

These needs may be present in most of the managers, but those with dominant need of any one of the above, will be highly successful in roles that suit this need, but may not be successful and may even fail in other roles.

vii. Goal setting theory: We will cover this last of the major theories here. It states that people are motivated to work hard and achieve the set goals if they are SMART (Specific, Measurable, Agreed upon, Realistic and Time-bound) and if they are given an action plan that will guide them and motivate them. We may add here that people's involvement will be greater if they also participate in this goal setting exercise. This will enable them to fulfil their needs as well as adhere to their values while they work towards achieving the goals.

6.2 Job Design:

As you can see from above theories, there is a mix of factors that act as motivators for individuals. From among these, as managers you need to choose and develop systems and procedures which are suitable to your organisational culture, corporate goals and values and your people. Based on these, your primary task will be to design jobs that meet with these factors in line with the systems and procedures. Some of the major considerations in designing jobs are discussed below:

i. Psychological contract: The starting point is the explicit and implicit contract between the organisation and the individual employee. In the formal contract, company's policies, systems and procedures are explicitly stated along with employment offer. The individual is expected to return a copy duly signed as a token of his/her acceptance of the terms mentioned therein.

What we are interested here is the implicit psychological contract made with the employee. Apart from the above explicitly stated norms, the employee is expected to behave in certain ways which are in line with the company's culture and traditions like openness, cooperation, sharing of information with colleagues, honesty, integrity etc. On its part, the organisation implicitly exhibits its commitment to these values. Other relational aspects also come into play.

ii.   Benefits of well-defined jobs: We will now move on to look at the benefits of well-defined jobs and factors that go into designing them. It is a fact that people will do their best in a job which they enjoy doing. Thus, a good job design leads to:

   •   A sense of fulfilment and achievement

   •   Feeling of doing a meaningful and worthwhile job

Job design primarily consists of putting together various tasks in a co-ordinated manner that the employee carries out so that a complete job is created. Though multi-tasking has become a buzz word these days, expecting a normal employee to carry out several "unrelated tasks" without a sense of completion may result in frustration.

iii.   The job characteristics model: As we know, in the early days of management as a discipline the accent of job design was primarily on increasing productivity. Mass production of interchangeable parts with assembly lines to maximise output was the driving force and the workers were beginning to feel like cogs in the wheels of a machine and became highly dissatisfied and demoralised. From around 1960, work study and redesign started to find ways to boost up employee satisfaction and thereby productivity by enriching jobs.

M/s. Hackman and Oldham developed their job characteristics model in the 1980s whose highlights are discussed in the following section.

iv. Five "core" job characteristics: The five core characteristics propounded by the model are: Skill variety, Task identity, Task significance, Autonomy and Feedback.

- Skill variety: By designing the job to consist of various activities that require worker to develop a variety of skills, you can make the employee feel that the job is meaningful.

- Task identity: Here, the completeness of job is important so that the job holder is involved in the entire process and it makes the job more meaningful.

- Task significance: The job should lead to outcomes that are seen as important to the group as well as to the organisation by the job holder.

- Autonomy: Here, the job provides significant freedom and discretion to the worker to plan the work and procedure involved. The job holder feels responsible for his/her own success or failure.

- Feedback: This involves giving clear feedback to the worker on results achieved and what specific actions are required to improve performance.

v. What a well-defined job offers to the employee's psychological state:

These are the psychological states the job holder experiences when doing a well-defined job as discussed in the previous section.

- Experienced meaningfulness of the work: The job holder feels as having done intrinsically meaningful work which he/she can present to others.

- Experienced responsibility for the outcome of work: The worker experiences his/her responsibility or accountability for the outcome.

- Knowledge of actual results of work: The worker gets to know how well he/she has performed with this knowledge.

vi. Outcomes of this approach to job design: The primary outcome of this approach to job design is high internal motivation that keeps the worker putting forth his/her best. Other benefits include quality and quantity of work turned out, less absenteeism etc. This model has undergone further refinements over the years with the objective of making jobs more meaningful, satisfactory and motivating. For those who are interested in exploring further, a Motivational Potential Score (MPS) for each job may be calculated by using scores to measure the potential score in each of the five core job characteristics.

vii. Job enrichment: All these concepts and practices are applied to enrich jobs to give greater satisfaction to employees. These efforts cover job enlargement initiatives and also job rotations so that the worker gets greater exposure and greater satisfaction in working for the organisation. These tend to be organisation specific.

viii. Motivating through continuous efforts towards enriching jobs in a changing world: We had earlier seen that the first steps in work redesign started in 1933 based on the Social Needs model developed by Prof. Elton Mayo. He postulated that people's social needs should be met for higher performance. The Socio Technical Systems approach was developed by three British professors at the

Tavistock Institute in London in 1951. It refers to the interaction between people and technology in workplaces. It emphasises on achieving excellence both in technical performance and people's work lives that leads to improved organisational performance.

This led to approaches like semi-autonomous group working, cellular organisations etc. Basically, in today's highly technology-driven and automated industrial world, repetitive jobs need to be humanised so that they are meaningful to workers. Further, emergence of higher proportion of white collar and knowledge workers have posed greater challenges in designing these jobs to make them meaningful and rewarding.

As we have been discussing, the bottom line is to improve employee involvement through greater empowerment whereby people own their jobs, excel in performance and get a sense of achievement and pride.

ix.   Current challenges:

•   "Work from Home": While it had been in vogue in a limited way especially in the IT industry for some time, the pandemic has brought in full force the necessity and inevitability of the practice of "work from home" in all jobs other than factory jobs where the physical presence of the worker is required. This has again posed great challenges to the organisations as well as employees in maintaining work performance as well as sense of belonging without physical presence with virtual meetings only.

•   "Work-life Balance": In a larger sense, a major challenge that is constantly faced by any worker- blue collar, white collar, technology or managerial employee is achieving an optimal work-life balance. While this has to be achieved by the individual, organisations do have a major role in enabling the employee to achieve this balance.

7.   Leadership:

We now move on to arguably the most important aspect of managing people- Leadership. It is the aim of every one of us to become a leader. Though there are differences in the requirements and characteristics between a manager and a leader, as we will see later, managers have to develop the necessary qualities to become a leader.

In this section we will look at various theories on leadership, functions of a leader, differences between management and leadership and finally look at leadership skills especially the communication skills.

As in the case of motivation and other people-related topics, there is no one best way to be a leader. You need to look at relevant points from each of these theories to arrive at your own requirements to become a great leader.

Your aim should be to move from a good leader to a great leader. Ultimately it is the collective effort of all people in the organisation that makes things happen and a great leader has to keep in mind this fact all the time. He/she has to ensure that people feel that they did it all by themselves rather than taking credit for the results achieved.

7.1   Theories of leadership:

As we know, leadership involves influencing others to follow a particular direction or goal. We can say that it is both an art and a science and leadership qualities are both in-born as well as can be developed.

Various theories of leadership can be broadly classified into:

- Trait theories
- Style theories
- Contingency theories

7.2 Trait theories:

These theories are based on the assumption that leaders have certain natural abilities which help them perform their leaderships roles in a natural way. Some of the major traits of successful leaders as given in any basic model of leadership are:

- Intelligence
- Interpersonal skills
- Self-confidence
- An orientation towards achievement
- A desire to play a dominant role in any situation

These are self-explanatory. As we had earlier seen under the learned need theory of motivation postulated by Dr. David McClelland, the primary motivating factors that drive leadership are:

- Need for achievement
- Need for affiliation
- Need for power

These motives are reflected in the trait theory of leadership in addition to the basic factors of intelligence and self-confidence.

While these traits are essential, any one dominant trait of a leader may not be suitable for all occasions and in all situations. In fact, a mismatch will result in crisis of leadership. A great leader needs to possess a balanced trait inventory so that he/she could adopt his/her style to meet the requirements of the emerging situation.

7.3   Style theories:

Here again, there are several theories highlighting different styles of operation by a leader. All these come under the umbrella of style theories and following are the major ones:

i.   The managerial grid (Blake and Moulton, 1952): This classifies leadership styles into 5 categories and can be easily understood when they are plotted on a graph. The two axes represent Concern for task/production on the X axis and Concern for people on the Y axis and following are the five types that emerge:

•   Country club management: This is where concern for people is high but concern for task/production is low. Here, avoidance of conflict and sense of good fellowship are considered more important with scant attention for task/production. It is obvious that such a style of leadership will fail in the business world, especially in a competitive situation. Until late nineties, we have several examples of such companies primarily British ones in India after freedom, which had to fold up.

•   Impoverished management: Under this style, there is concern neither for people nor for task/production. Companies under this style also fold up sooner than later. Absentee owners and unconcerned senior managers follow this style.

•   Task management: "Produce somehow" is the mantra here and targets alone matter. Workers are treated as cogs in the wheel of production. This was the implicit style in the early days of so-called scientific management when sellers' markets prevailed and productivity alone was the aim of management.

- Team management: This is probably the most preferred style of management especially in modern times where ultimately human resources are considered as the most important resource. Here, the leader achieves high involvement of people by considering and catering to their individual, group and social needs and at the same time ensuring that tasks are carried out as planned and production/targets are achieved. Thus, they exhibit a very high concern for both people and task/production.

- Dampened pendulum: This is the style adopted by leaders who believe that they can give a little care to people and also care a little for task/production. "Give some and take some" or "be firm and fair" are often used cliches here and the company remains in stagnant, suspended mode neither progressing forward nor demise. "Status quo" is maintained until it is taken over and revived.

This is a very influential theory and leaders are often labelled as "autocratic", "democratic and participative", "weak and apathetic", "status quoist" or "jolly good fellow" based on their style of leadership.

ii.   The Tannenbaum and Schmidt continuum (1973): Various leadership styles named after the original authors mentioned above, are represented as a continuum with the highest use of authority at one end and giving maximum freedom to sub-ordinates in a decision-making process at the other end.

The various styles are:

- "Tells": The leader/manager takes all decisions
- "Sells": The leader "sells" the decisions through persuasion

- "Tests": He/she presents the ideas and tests them with sub-ordinates
- "Suggests": The difference here is that the leader suggests a way forward to be modified as required
- Consults: The leader presents the problems, gets suggestions and makes the decisions
- Joins: The parameters are defined and the leader works with the group to find the solution
- Delegates: The leader sets the limits for sub-ordinates and delegates the decision-making to them

While it is obvious that the optimum preferred style is involving team members in decision-making, the leader has to understand the nature of the problem and adopt the appropriate style in decision-making. It is akin to "team management" style.

iii. Contingency theories of leadership styles: These are based on the underlying premises of larger contingency models which can be shortly summarised as "it all depends". Here, we can say that successful leadership depends on the situation. We will take a look at one of the well-known contingency theories based on Fiedler's matrix of management styles.

Prof. Fiedler has postulated that preferred individual leadership style is based on the individual leader, the organisational factors which can be called as leadership situation and the interaction between these factors and leadership style.

The leadership style is grouped into task-oriented and relationship-oriented, similar to Blake and Moulton's grid.

The organisational factors or leadership situation can be grouped into three major components:

- Leader-member relations
- Task structure
- Position power

We can classify leader-member relations into good, moderate or poor as follows:

- Good: where the leader is familiar and comfortable with competence and commitment levels of sub-ordinates and they in turn believe in his/her competence and like him/her
- Moderate: when both and neutral or indifferent
- Poor: when the leader as well as sub-ordinates neither have confidence in competence nor commitment of each other

We can again classify task structure into high, medium or low based on how complex the task is and the degree to which a detailed plan of execution is in place.

Position power of the leader refers to the degree to which he/she can exercise authority on sub-ordinates which could be high, medium or low.

Putting all this together, we can arrive at the overall leadership situation. Matching this with the leadership style, the theory advocates effective style as follows:

Leadership situation	Effective style
Favourable	Task orientation
Intermediate	Relationship orientation
Unfavourable	Task orientation

This illustrates that when the leader has either of the styles as his/her preferred personal style, he/she often fails in situations which are not favourable to this style. Corporate world is littered with several "so-called" great leaders whose styles often undermined the effectiveness of the organisation.

When there is a situation which demands immediate action and the group is indecisive, the leader has to be "task-oriented" and ensure timely implementation taking control of the situation. On the other hand, when there are multiple problems and different points of view need to be considered, a "relationship oriented" or participative style is preferred.

All these discussions go only to show that the leader has to have the maturity, knowledge and the will to lead as per the demands of the situation to take the team with him/her.

7.4   Leadership functions:

We have seen that leadership consists of involving others to follow a particular direction or goal. To carry out his/her leadership role effectively, a leader needs to perform several functions. These can be broadly classified into:

- Strategic function
- Task function
- Interpersonal function

i.   Strategic function: The primary function of a leader is to develop a sense of direction in the group or in the organisation. This consists of several steps as listed below:

- Analysis of the business environment
- Setting the vision, mission and goals for the organisation in line with company's values, strengths and weaknesses

- Communicating these effectively to all members
- Ensuring that they understand and follow the guidelines to achieve these goals

The importance of setting the strategic direction as the primary function can never be overemphasised. What differentiates a successful leader is his/her ability to lead the group and the organisation in the right path for success.

ii. Task function: Once the direction has been set, the leader has to develop the necessary plan of action to execute in achievement of goals. This consists of

- Developing necessary organisation and assigning duties and responsibilities for key personnel and their teams
- Defining tasks to be performed by each of these members and their teams
- Finalising resources required and arranging for these
- Creating necessary systems and procedures to control operations and monitoring results
- Ensuring effective implementation of strategy and overall plans
- Dealing with emergencies and adverse developments in time

These involve considering all aspects of finance, marketing and operations functions.

iii. Interpersonal function: Often it is said that motivating people and ensuring their performance are the primary functions of leadership. These involve following steps:

- Communicating clearly and effectively the strategic direction of the company openly to all employees

- Getting their whole-hearted commitment
- Providing necessary motivation for them to own up the responsibilities and excel in their performance
- Maintaining morale of the people at all times
- Ensuring cohesion and teamwork among people

Thus, the leadership functions consist of a complex set of activities relating to strategy, task and people related functions. Ultimately, the leader should own up his role and ensure that "the buck stops here" with him/her at the helm.

7.5 Leaders and managers:

Before we move on to discussing skills required for effective leadership, we will briefly look at the differences between leaders and managers. Some of them clearly distinguish what a successful leader does from what a manager does. In others, there are only subtle differences on the emphasis placed.

Leader	Manager
Inventor and initiator of original ideas and actions	Primarily an administrator of the path laid
Emphasis on building teams and focus on people	More emphasis on systems and procedures and task
Inspires people to follow	Control is the main focus to get things done
Takes a long-range perspective and develops a vision	Concerned about short-term objectives
Raises basic questions on what and when to do	Primarily interested in how we are doing and why
challenges the status quo	Accepting given circumstances or status quo
Ultimately decides and accepts responsibility "The buck stops here"	Expects orders to be given and carries them out

You should not get into the exercise of splitting hair on what leader does and what manager does. They are often overlapping and, in many instances, the leader acts as a manager as well and vice versa.

Prof. Fenton O' Creevy of the Open University Business School, UK, summarises the difference as follows:

"Leadership is concerned with creating goals, giving a sense of direction and gaining commitment of other people to these goals. Management can be thought of as a process of organising people and resources to achieve given goals."

7.6 The hallmarks of a great leader:

As we saw earlier, the whole thrust here is how to move up from being a good leader to a great leader since most of you in your work situations, play leadership roles in some aspects of your activities. We list out some of the ways of great leaders that enable them to achieve great results.

i. Inspiring a shared vision among people: By far, this may be the most important characteristic of a great leader. One may call it charisma, but people just follow this vision.

ii. Appealing to hearts: As a corollary, we can say that these leaders' appeal to the hearts of people is greater than pure rational approach.

iii. Empowering: The great leader empowers and enables others to act in achievement of this vision with a firm belief that collective effort alone will yield the best results.

iv. Leading by example: Of course, the great one leads by example which further reinforces the trust in him/her. They literally "walk the talk".

v.   Challenging the status quo: As we saw just now, he/she always challenges the status quo and constantly looks for newer avenues and newer ways of working.

7.7   Leadership primary skill set:

While we normally expect leaders to be "superhuman beings" and masters of all kinds of skills, some important skills they normally possess are as follows:

i.   They are great communicators: Often, leaders are able to articulate their vision clearly and effectively to their audience, viz. people in the organisation and outsiders which makes the required impact on the receivers.

ii. Charisma, actions and behaviour: By virtue of their charisma, and through their actions and behaviour, great leaders are able to maintain the morale, cohesion and commitment of the group for the shared vision.

iii. Action orientation: Added to these are their action orientation which leads to a culture of execution- "doing things", rather than just developing strategies and action plans. This decisiveness is important in demonstrating their commitment to the common cause or vision.

iv. "Lead by example": This is another admirable characteristic of great leaders. They do not just stop with preaching but demonstrate by following the path themselves. They do "walk the talk".

v.   Acting as ambassadors: They act as the voice of the group or organisation and represent it to the outside world as ambassadors. Thus, they create the necessary image of the organisation.

This list is in no way exhaustive. As we saw, contingent upon the emerging situation the leader may have to employ further skills to achieve the set objectives even as she/he takes all people along.

7.8 The skill of communication:

While communication skills are essential in all walks of life including in your daily interactions, these are fundamental to a leader since leadership involves communicating his/her vision and chosen path to the members of the organisation and inspiring and influencing them to follow that path. Hence special coverage here. The basic components of communication consist of the message and the media and with constantly evolving communication technology, there is a need for the leader to keep himself/herself abreast of all latest developments and become familiar with them be it through conventional speech, writing, mail, video conferencing or social media. Our primary emphasis here is on the broader requirements for effective communication.

i.   Creating necessary climate for open communication: It is the responsibility of the leader to ensure that the communication climate is open and supportive. Only this will elicit open and honest responses. This culture of open and supportive communication is essential to convey rational solutions as well as deal with emotional conflicts in the organisation as a whole or in smaller groups. On the other hand, a closed climate will lead to biases, suspicion, non-caring and hostile behaviour.

The communication climate can further lead to either adversarial or cooperative relationships both in large and small groups. This is very much in the hands of the leader since he/she sets the communication climate and nurtures it through own example by being open and honest.

ii. Communicating through presentations (oral and written): Often, it is through formal meetings in large or small groups that the leader conveys his/her ideas, plans and directives to the members of the organisation, customers or clients and even government officials. Of course, with the Covid 19 pandemic continuing to rage all over the world, most of such meetings and presentations are done virtually through online platforms. Here, we will list some of the points that help in making effective presentations. These are largely for oral presentations but similar tips are applicable for written communication as well.

- Preparing for presentation: Basically, you should know and understand your audience, their requirements and level of comprehension. For example, there is really no point in delivering a top notch, crisp presentation in high-flown language when your target audience may be primarily used to day-to-day spoken and written language.

- You can take it as an axiom that a communication is effective only when the receiver understands the message exactly as the leader intended to convey. This should always be kept in mind in any communication process.

- Of course, it goes without saying that you need to be prepared with the following:

i. The purpose and the content

ii. Structure

iii. Delivery style

- During presentation: While the tone and tenor of your voice or delivery are important, other non-verbal cues may be noted during oral presentations

i.   Physical and facial expression

ii. Posture

iii. Eye contact

iv. Gestures

In written communication, you need to also take care of the tone and tenor of your writing, clarity of thought and emotional content as well.

iii. Interpersonal communication: Often, in one-to-one or interpersonal communication, there are other challenges as well. These come up especially when you give feedback on the performance of a person reporting to you. While good work should be appreciated and encouraged, you should also specifically point out the areas where the performance of the individual has exceeded on agreed upon objectives and areas where he can do better. On the other hand, when you have to give feedback on poor performance, the challenges are greater. While you have to make an honest assessment of the person's performance and be prepared to answer points he may raise, you have to be equally honest and open while giving the feedback. We will see more on this later in section on Managing performance.

8. Primary functions of Human Resources Management Department (HRM):

We have just covered the important aspects of Motivation and Leadership which are fundamental to any organisation to be successful. We now move on to the core functions to be carried out as part of Human Resources Management (HRM) department which are governed by standard policies, systems and procedures of the organisation. These consist of:

- Managing entry or recruitment of people
- Performance management, primarily importance of performance monitoring and reward systems
- Managing development of people

While these may come specifically under core functions of HRM department, every manager/leader has to be actively involved and consulted while framing the necessary systems and procedures covering these functions and in implementing them consistently to create a world-class organisation. We have seen that the immediate supervisor or manager is the first point of contact for the employee and he/she is seen to represent company's policies and practices in managing human resources.

8.1 Managing entry:

i. Steps involved in managing entry of people into the organisation are:

- Analysing jobs, people requirements, designing and developing job descriptions
- Recruitment and selection: There is a minor difference between these two processes. Recruitment involves calling for and attracting suitable candidates for the job to be filled. This is done through word-of-mouth, direct advertising or through recruitment agencies, consultants etc.

ii. Selection of candidates for the job consists of several steps like

- Application forms to be obtained from the candidate to get complete details of qualifications, job experience, present salary drawn, references, job preferences etc

- Reference checks to verify the details provided. Very often, people tend to misrepresent facts or overstate their qualifications and work experience
- Personal interviews by a panel of interviewers
- Personality, aptitude/attitude tests etc
- Making the offer to the selected candidate and get his/her acceptance.

iii. Induction: Finally, it is a part of entry process to arrange for the recruited candidate to go through an induction process. This is to give the new entrant an opportunity to get familiar with the job for which he/she has been recruited, company's policies, systems and procedures governing employment. The new person will also get to know the immediate boss, colleagues and other important members of the organisation. During this process, he/she will also get a feel of the organisation's culture and get used to it.

iv. Selecting the right candidate: There are some major points to be considered in final selection of the candidate as given below:

- As we saw, after developing the job description based on the organisational and job requirements, you need to develop a set of specifications for the candidate. This will include his/her educational background, work experience etc.

- From the list of applicants short-listed, you could further refine through personality or other tests.

- Often, interviews are the most commonly accepted method of selection. While several tips are available for the candidate, as far as the interview panel is concerned, they need to avoid biases of any sort.

- Very often, the recruiters get carried away positively or negatively at the first look based on candidate's records, physical appearance, tone and tenor of replies etc. They tend to build on these impressions called the "halo" or "horn" effect which should be avoided. This is applicable in all cases of personal interview- face-to-face, through video conferencing which is the practice in these days of the pandemic or even telephonic interviews.
- The panel members need to be honest and satisfy themselves on their decision.
- An important consideration is to decide whether you are looking for a person who will "fit" the job and/or "fit" with the organisation's culture. There may be divergences here.

8.2 Managing performance:

We will look at performance management under three sub-headings:

- Importance of supervision
- Giving feedback and conducting appraisal interviews
- Pay and reward systems

i. Effective supervision and support: We have seen that very often the immediate supervisor/boss is the most important contact person for an employee in the organisation. The supervisor's activities can be grouped into task-related and person/people- oriented activities.

Task-oriented activities would include:

- Explaining company's objectives and setting targets
- Resourcing the person for the tasks to be performed
- Guiding the employee for better performance

- Keeping a check on adherence to systems, procedures and limits thereof while at the same time, delegating more tasks

Person-oriented activities consist of:

- Facilitating performance through providing guidance and encouragement
- Counselling and coaching
- Representing the employee's interests to higher-ups in the organisation
- Evaluating, recognising and rewarding performance by words and deeds and recommending other rewards and special recognitions as per company's rewards policies

Often, supervisors fall into the trap of either over supervision or under supervision. Also, they start overloading good performers subconsciously and may at times be not consistent in their approach. Hence, a supervisor needs to be consistent, carry out both task-related and people-oriented supervision and act as the employees' spokesperson.

ii. Setting individual performance standards: We know that only what gets measured, gets done. Hence, the need for both task-related as well as behavioural-related standards of performance.

- A basic requirement is that the employee adheres to the standards set in terms of time of work, attendance, leave rules etc as specified in the appointment contract letter. Normally, organisations have automated systems for recording these for both blue-collar and white-collar workers, but still certain amount of supervisory intervention is required in terms of sanctioning of leave, giving time-off for urgent work and the like. In the case of managerial staff, the culture of the organisation comes into play. In the present times, the Covid 19 pandemic has upended all conventional practices in terms of hours and place of work, reporting, supervision etc so much that we may never get back to the old practices in the near future. Work from home itself is the single most important disruptor of the conventional office system and both employers and employees are yet to get fully adjusted to this major change.

- Quantity of output is measured against standards in terms of quantity, time, cost etc for evaluating quantitative performance.

- Quality of finished work, upkeep of work area, record maintenance, promptness and quality of reporting etc are the qualitative measures used normally in evaluating quality of work done by the employee. While these seem to be applicable largely for blue-collar employees, similar parameters help in the case of white-collar employees as well. Again, during these days, how well the person prepares and presents his/her work during video conferencing etc need to be looked at.

These qualitative and quantitative measures can be measured against standards and targets and by instituting regular reporting systems and procedures.

iii. Measuring behavioural performance: This is a difficult area. Following measures are used:

- Unpleasant behaviour with customers, colleagues and supervisors

- Being dishonest or indulging in spreading wrong rumours

- Converting minor issues into organisation-wide major ones

These are some of the negative points. Employees who do not indulge in such disruptive practices and who have a positive attitude towards colleagues, work and organisation and being helpful when necessary are the traits of good behavioural performance.

These factors are rather difficult to measure and certain amount of subjective judgment of the supervisor goes into measuring and giving feedback on these aspects.

iv. Some critical aspects of giving feedback: We will now look at the two related areas of dealing with under-performance and giving feedback during formal performance appraisals.

- In both cases, the supervisor and the appraiser need to be honest, have their facts and appraisals ready with them.

- They should hold the interview in a congenial atmosphere for free and frank exchange, avoiding all pitfalls like biases on any kind.

- They should be objective and not compare the performance of the employee and other colleagues.

- They should limit their feedback and appraisal to present performance only and not indulge in speaking about past performance.

- Finally, they should develop a mutually agreed way forward for improving employee's performance where necessary.

8.3 Developing and implementing rewards system:

From the employee's point of view, a critical factor in joining and continuing with an organisation and get committed to its goal, is its pay and rewards system. We will now go through the major considerations in developing a sound rewards or compensation policy.

i. Basic premise: You know that people make organisations. Any organisation can work effectively in the long term only when needs of individual employees are fulfilled as they work together to achieve the set objectives. This forms the basic premise on which organisations hire/employ people. They in turn, join the organisation with the understanding that their expectations will be met when they perform their tasks as expected and agreed upon. The terms of employment normally list out the duties and responsibilities of each position as well as pay and rewards parameters for that position and the individual.

ii. Major aspects of pay and rewards system: Given this background, the HR department in consultation with top management, develops and implements the pay and reward policies, systems and procedures. Some of the major factors considered in developing a sound system are as given below:

*   Organisation's size, market position, financial status, reputation etc

*   Comparison with market rates for similar jobs in comparable organisations. This is based on equity theory of motivation.

*   Within the organisation, individual jobs are evaluated and an equitable salary and rewards structure is finalised. This is monitored continuously with other similar organisations and competitors.

iii. Different payment systems: Different companies follow different payment systems based on nature of industry, labour market conditions, their specific requirements etc. Some of the common payment systems are listed below:

- Fixed flat rates based on time, for example, daily wages, monthly salaries etc
- Piece rates where output can be directly measured, primarily for production workers
- Yearly increments based on time scale and/or performance review of results
- Performance related payment systems and special increments based on merit
- Special qualifications obtained and training underwent while in service with the company, where such factors lead to better performance. This is also as a part of individual development and promotion plans for positions of greater responsibility

iv. Rewards systems- summary: Summing up, we can say that employees in general, tend to compare what they get with what they bring in. They have a measure of what they get as their total compensation in terms of pay, perquisites, long term benefits etc, recognition of good performance, greater sense of belonging, freedom and responsibility etc. They also have a feel of what they bring in to their job and organisation in terms of their qualifications and skills, outputs they deliver, taking on responsibilities, exhibiting a sense of solidarity with company's goals etc. If they are satisfied with what they get as an adequate compensation for all the inputs they have brought in, they are generally satisfied with the system. In addition, they also compare what they get with what others are getting within the organisation and outside for comparable positions to judge the fairness of the system. As often said, you as the manager, not only need to be fair, but also need to be seen to be fair.

8.4 Managing Development- Developing people:

Among other major areas, developing people at all levels on an ongoing basis occupies a central role in ensuring robust, long-term well-being of the organisation and hence should be a part and parcel of every manager's job. It is the duty of top management to ensure that systems and procedures are in place to monitor the development activities regularly.

i. Competencies as the basis for high performance: As a manager, you are responsible for the development of people reporting to you. We saw right at the beginning that people are the only assets of an organisation that do not depreciate over a period of time. In fact, they can be developed to perform more activities and take on greater responsibilities. In the ultimate analysis, human assets are the most critical assets of an organisation. While the other assets by themselves may not be of use when the organisation needs a total transformation of its business, only people have the flexibility and can make this transformation possible. Hence, developing people is an essential requirement for developing the organisation continuously in terms of new products, new markets and totally new business opportunities.

ii. Basic competences: At a broad level, we can say that competences refer to the basic requirements for a person to perform effectively in the job which has been assigned to him/her. These are minimum entry standards of task-oriented knowledge and skills required. When we expect higher levels of performance and capabilities to move up to the next levels in terms of managing people, we need people to possess competencies which can often be developed if the candidate has the necessary aptitude and attitude. Often, the difference between competence and competency is just semantic and both words are used interchangeably.

Basic competences can be grouped into:

- Industry/trade-specific competences
- Technical competences specific to industry and the organisation

iii. Meta competencies: Going beyond technical, industry and organisation-specific competencies, managers have to look for what can be called as meta competencies in further developing themselves and people reporting to them. These are required for achieving high levels of performance and also for equipping oneself for positions of higher responsibilities, managerial and leadership positions. These can be broadly grouped under the following:

- Competency for information searching, gathering and analytical capabilities. These are of critical importance in to-day's fast-developing, information-driven business environment. The person should be able to decide what information is relevant, know where to look for it, gather and analyse the data and information so gathered.

- Creativity is yet another competency to look at problems and opportunities from different perspectives and arrive at solutions. This is called "out of box thinking".

- People competencies in terms of ability to communicate, co-operate, negotiate and influence people. These are hallmarks of outstanding managers and leaders.

- In times of crisis and uncertainty like the time we are in right now thanks to the onslaught of relentless pandemic, a great manager/leader needs to work with uncertainty and take decisions based on imperfect information and an uncertain future.

- Finally, it goes without saying that other meta competencies like self-confidence, action and result orientation and a high degree of empathy- all differentiate highly successful managers and leaders from others.

iv. Training and Development (T & D): Though Training and Development are generally used together and also as synonyms, there is a subtle difference in their approach.

- Training is usually applicable for all efforts aimed at helping an individual upgrade his/her skills in a particular task or activity, with all latest technological and other advances in carrying out these tasks. Examples include upgrading a worker's skills in using modern digital technologies for greater efficiency.

- Development on the other hand means helping and preparing individuals to take on greater responsibilities by broadening their knowledge and skills base consisting of people management skills, analysis and problem-solving skills and at higher levels, decision making and working under uncertain conditions capabilities etc. Normally, people who have the potential to move up to more responsible positions and who need to develop skills other than their own job/function specific competencies, are selected to undergo suitable development programmes. For example, a production manager may undergo a development programme in financial management fundamentals that are essential for a position like plant manager etc.

Having said that, we will use both these together as means to developing people for higher skill levels, more skill sets and broader understanding in other business functional areas.

v.   Your role as a manager in training and development: As a line manager, you have to play a leading role in many ways in the training and development of people reporting to you, as listed below:

  • During your routine supervisory performance review interactions, you are best placed to offer advice to them on improving their performance.

  • You can expose them to opportunities to practise newer skills.

  • As "gate-keeper", you can offer them other opportunities for off-the-job training and development by recommending their names to the organisation for sponsoring them to special programmes etc.

vi. Options available for training and development:

  • Coaching and mentoring: These are readily available. A coach is generally a specialist who can offer specific skills. A mentor is often a senior manager, not the direct boss of the employee, who is interested in the overall development and offer advice and guidance on a periodic basis.

  • Job rotations: This will equip the person to understand requirements to perform different jobs and make him/her a well-rounded performer.

  • Involving the employee in special assignments.

  • You can co-opt the employee for special assignments like project studies, new product development either individually or as a member of a team which is called as specific task force.

- In-house courses by trainers/ developers within the organisation.

- Sponsorship to external courses both practical and academic, to broaden their horizon.

- The last two are often for developing and preparing people for positions of higher responsibilities.

vii. Measuring effectiveness of training and development: Only in specific skill-oriented training programmes, their effectiveness can be directly measured. In other development programmes which involve learning new fields and developing more inclusive skills and competencies, it is often difficult to measure the impact of the programmes immediately or directly.

The bottom line is that any training or development programme will succeed only with whole-hearted commitment of both direct line mangers and top management who should believe in the basic idea that the programme so organised is essential. All the programmes should be well conceived, details, contents and methodologies worked out and delivered in the most efficient manner.

9. Developing self:

We have often seen that the business environment has always been dynamic, more so now with rapid development of technologies, globalisation, changing demographics and constantly evolving consumer preferences. The pace of change is so fast that unless you keep yourself updated with all the latest development, generally in the business environment and more so in your own industry, you will be left behind and will not be able to cope. Always keep in mind that developing yourself continuously is your own responsibility.

Life-long employment is a past story and you need to develop your knowledge and skills constantly to have greater freedom to act and greater mobility. On the other hand, this current trend of "information overload" makes your job even more daunting and more challenging since you need to develop the necessary insight to distinguish reliable information from unreliable ones. These lead to greater pressure on you to perform and you, in turn, get stressed out and feel worried and left out. Let us start with looking at pressure and stress before moving on to avenues for developing yourself.

9.1 Pressure and stress:

Pressure is from external sources whereas stress is your internal response. As a manager, these forces are more severe since you are also responsible for the work done by others. Furthermore, your role may not have clear boundaries and striking a balance between work and home becomes more difficult. Yet again, the "pressure" of working from home due to the pandemic has exacerbated your stress even further. The trick lies in handling pressure confidently and not getting stressed over it.

9.2 Career anchor:

A good way to plan for developing yourself will be to decide what you consider is the primary "career anchor" for you which is consistent with your values, attitudes and strengths. Prof. Edgar Schein, American professor, has listed eight such anchors one of which may be the primary driving force in your career building/life style efforts. They are:

• Technical/functional expertise: If you want to be an outstanding professional in your field.

- Entrepreneurial creativity: For those who are creative and have original ideas which they want to convert into business venture

- General management competence: Apart from being analytical with a problem-solving bent of mind, these people have the competence to develop their "emotional intelligence" about which we will see later.

- Service/dedication: For many social entrepreneurs and workers, the driving force is their all-pervasive desire to be of service to community etc.

- Autonomy/Independence: Such people do not want to report to others, preferring to do things in their own ways.

- Pure challenge: These people like a job just for the heck of pure challenge that it offers. They look for challenging jobs and thrive well when they meet new challenges.

- Security/stability: These are the driving forces for persons who want minimal disruption and prefer to lead a secure and stable life.

- Life style: If you are a person driven by your passion for a particular life style/hobby etc, this may be your anchor. You may be able to achieve life/work balance with a bias towards a satisfactory life style.

9.3 Planning for self-development:

Some of the major factor you must consider in your plans for self-development are:

- As mentioned just above, plan your career moves based on your career anchor.

- Adopt learning methods that suit your learning style.

- Get to know your employer's needs, culture and style and see whether they meet with the requirements of your career anchor. For a person who prefers autonomy/ independence, a centrally-driven autocratic culture and style may not be suitable.

• Develop your skills to think critically which will help you in planning your development needs.

• Make life-long learning a habit and keep adding to your knowledge and skills that will enhance your repertoire.

• Above all, keep moving forward constantly in your self-development efforts.

9.4 Emotional intelligence:

While emotional intelligence or EQ is most important to be successful in all walks of life, it is especially so for leadership and managerial positions. Hence this special mention of EQ as essential part of your self-development plans. Emotional intelligence consists of mastering your own self as well as effectively dealing with others for successful relationships. While the classic IQ or Intelligence Quotient and technical skills form the basic threshold competencies, EQ is essential for effective leadership.

The idea of EQ was made popular in 1995 by Mr. Daniel Goleman, author and researcher in the USA and has become one of the most important topics in leadership essentials. Mr. Goleman has defined EQ as consisting of following five components:

• Self-awareness

• Self-regulation

• Motivation

• Empathy

• Social skills

The first three form part of managing self and the latter two refer to managing interactions with others.

i. Self-awareness: This consists of understanding self and one's own moods, emotions, drives etc and their effect on others. People who have mastered self-awareness, develop self-confidence based on their self-assessment.

ii. Self-regulation: Having achieved self-awareness, a good leader should be able to control his/her moods etc and act only after judging the impact of their actions on others. He/she becomes open to change and is also able to earn the trust of others.

iii. Motivation: We can recall our discussions on various theories of motivation in this context. Great leaders strive for self-realisation. It is the need for achievement that drives them.

iv. Empathy: It is the ability to put oneself in the shoes of others and understand their points of view. This enables them to manage meaningful relationships, help people as needed and build effective teams.

v. Social skill: This further leads to mutually beneficial relationships and helps in inspiring people and managing change.

We may say that all these skills can be developed, while they may come naturally to those with strong leadership traits.

9.5 Your role in developing yourself:

All the above discussions would confirm that developing self is primarily your own responsibility. You have to devote quality time and effort in this direction on a continuing basis. Two things are worth mentioning here. They are: Action learning and Reflective practice which are two sides of life-long learning since learning never stops.

Action learning refers to learning from experience. Reflective practice refers to the process of analysing the outcomes of your actions and modify or add on to your repertoire of your values, ideas, knowledge and skills. In addition, you can always resort to learning from formal training, mentors and role models.

10. Learning organisation:

We will now move on to creating and sustaining a learning organisation which enables its members to embark on this journey of continuous development. Prof. Peter Senge of USA has outlined the characteristics of learning organisations in his book, "The fifth Discipline". These are:

- Systems thinking- the fifth discipline
- Personal mastery
- Mental models
- Shared vision
- Team learning

i. Systems thinking: This is called the fifth discipline which a learning organisation exhibits after mastering the other four. It enables people to look at the organisation as a whole system where there are systems in place to measure the total performance as well as individual components. This leads to open and continuous learning. It is a continuing process.

ii. Personal mastery: Here, every individual is committed to continuous learning and self-improvement. This paves the way for collective organisational learning leading to learning organisation.

iii. Mental models: All of us have our own mental models that lead to what are called espoused theories, but what we actually put into practice are called theories-in-use. We need to challenge our hidden mental models or espoused theories as well as theories-in-use to discard what are unsuitable as part of our learning process so that we can re-learn what are necessary for evolving environment. Same is the case with an organisation that questions its current business policies and practices for adopting newer ones. This is evident in the current situation where the emerging digital business environment is forcing organisations to rethink their whole approach to doing business to stay relevant to their customers.

iv. Shared vision: It goes without saying that creating a shared vision is fundamental to a learning organisation that provides focus and energy for learning to the individuals.

v. Team learning: Again, collection of individual learning leads to team learning. This is facilitated by cross learning by frank exchange of ideas and actions leading to learning from one another.

10. Managing change:

It is a cliche' to say that change is the only constant in the present business environment. Change is all pervasive in all types of organisations, big or small, at team/group level, departmental level company level and corporate level.

In any change situation, there are people who initiate change and some of the employees who readily accept the challenge of change. There are others who are directly or indirectly affected and are sceptical about change. As a leader/manager, in most cases you will be the change initiator or change implementor. Often, change may become necessary due to changes in the external environment. A thorough analysis of some of the basic factors to be considered in initiating change are as follows:

- Interconnectedness of various components of the organisation
- Factors driving or blocking change called force-field analysis
- The change process itself

10.1 Deciding on whether to change or not:

In any organisation, an analysis based on "Diamond of interconnectedness of organisation" developed by Prof. Harold Levitt will be useful. He has highlighted four components which are interconnected that define an organisation. Any change in any one of these, will affect others as well as the whole organisation. They are:

- People
- Structures
- Systems and technology
- Tasks

It is obvious that any change you contemplate in any one of these components will have a cascading effect. Hence before embarking on a change project in any one of these areas, its effect on all other areas and the organisation as a whole, should be studied. If the benefits outweigh the adverse impact, plans should be in place to address the possible consequences.

10.2 Driving and restraining forces in a change situation:

Elaborating on this, in any change situation there are certain forces which may be driving the change like your leadership, technological changes, people changes etc. There will be corresponding restraining forces which may impede change and may even derail the process. Classic example will be when in a public sector undertaking, there is a crying need for upgrading technology, it may be met with fierce opposition from employees. This analysis should help in anticipating both driving forces and the opposing forces and develop plans and strategies for implementation.

10.3 The change process:

The change process can be grouped into three phases:

- Phase 1: Preparing for change (called unfreezing)
- Phase 2: Implementing change (moving change)
- Phase 3: Consolidating change (refreezing)

Each phase has several steps which need to be planned and executed so that the organisation moves forward in the desired direction after all the phases are completed.

Under phase 1, communication is the key. People have to be informed of the proposed change and reasons calling for change. Apart from enlisting the support of persons who will welcome the proposed change, concerns of those resisting it and who are likely to be adversely impacted need to be addressed in an honest and frank dialogue. One strategy would be to start with initial steps that will find greater acceptance by affected people or groups.

During the implementation phase, phase 2, a great deal of time should be spent in planning all steps and putting in place necessary systems for implementation and follow up. Contingency plans should be ready to meet any unexpected developments.

Finally, during the consolidating phase, phase 3, all steps should be taken to ensure that changes effected stick and are continuously monitored until they become new ways of working.

Most of the change initiatives, big or small, often fail primarily because all factors have not been fully considered and also because other totally unforeseen developments take place. Change, at the individual level, group level and organisation level, is a challenging process and the mettle of a great leader is in getting the support of all employees affected and driving the change process successfully. It is a fact that often the desired changes do not take place fully and results achieved do not meet the objectives in full measure. Also very soon, it will be time for yet another change in this fast-paced environment.

10.4 Effecting major change in a large corporation:

Finally, I would like to discuss a specific model for implementing changes in large corporations. As we just saw, most of the major change efforts in large organisations fail. American Change and Leadership professor and management consultant Kotter has proposed an 8-step change model for achieving greater success in major change initiatives in large organisations. Though some of them may be culture and country specific, Indian corporations both in public and private sectors will find this model of immense use in their change efforts. The eight steps proposed by Prof. Kotter are:

i.   Create a sense of urgency

ii.   Create a guiding coalition

iii. Create a vision for change

iv.   Communicate the vision

v.   Remove the obstacles

vi.   Celebrate short term wins

vii. Consolidate improvements

viii. Anchor the changes

These steps are self-explanatory. You can see that the first three steps refer to Phase-1, Preparing for change mentioned in the previous section. Steps 4 to 6 form Phase-2, Implementing change and steps 7 & 8 correspond to Phase-3, Consolidating change. While specific actions to be taken under each step may depend on circumstances, this model presents overall guidelines to ensure that all necessary steps are considered and taken so that chances of ensuring success of the desired change initiatives are enhanced.

In my view, there are two important points to be kept in mind to ensure success of major change strategies in organisations. As we just saw in the beginning of this chapter, change is the only constant in this ever-changing business environment and there will be continuing need for effecting changes in all companies.

- As we can see, it is the duty of the topmost management viz. the leader to initiate, nurture and follow-up on the major change initiatives affecting the whole organisation. Total commitment and involvement of the leader is essential, and he/she should "walk the talk" and lead by example. It goes without saying that the leader has to take the entire team of people with him/her during all stages of this change process.

- Even after change process is complete, the leader and the senior management team can never afford to rest on their laurels since they have to be constantly vigilant and keep scanning the environment both proactively and reactively to be ready for the next change.

In conclusion, we can say that it is most appropriate to end this booklet on HRM with the topic of Managing Change, though it may be an oxymoron. More often than not, organisations only react to changes that are constantly taking place in the larger business and economic environment. At best, successful organisations anticipate likely changes and are ready to meet the challenges of change and take all their people along the change path. As we saw, ultimately, it is people who make organisations and hence, Managing Change is a crucial part of managing people.

Primary reference books

1. Study Materials for B-800: Foundations of Senior Management By the Open University Business School, UK

2. Marketing 3.0: From Products to Customers to the Human Spirit (2010) By Philip Kotler, Hermawan and Iwan Setiawan

3. Marketing Management: A South Asian Perspective (13th Edition - 2009) By Philip Kotler, Kevin Lane Keller, Abraham Koshy and Mithileshwar Jha

4. Strategic Brand Management: Building, Measuring and Managing Brand Equity (2nd Edition - 2007) By Kevin Lane Keller

5. Mastering Management 2.0: Your Single-Source Guide to Becoming a Master of Management By Financial Times: Edited by James Pickford (2004)

6. Organisational behaviour (11th Edition - 2006) By Stephen P. Robbins and Seema Sanghi

7. Key management ratios: The 100+ ratios every manager needs to know (Fourth edition - 2008) By Ciaran Walsh

8. Contemporary Strategy Analysis (Third Edition - 1998) By Robert M. Grant

Afterword

I started writing the booklet on Basics of Business Management and subsequent booklets covering each block by end of 2019. So far, I have completed four booklets and two more remain. The Covid 19 pandemic hit the world right through this period of end 2019, whole of 2020, 2021 and third and fourth waves are on us right now since January 2022. It has shaken the very basics of our lives to a great extent. As a consequence, whatever is written here has to be seen in this changed context. While all the basic and classic ideas presented here are equally applicable in the present circumstances, we need to modify the ways in which we apply them in the present context.

For example, work from home and online meetings have become the new norms in inter and intra office meetings involving white collar jobs. However, one can see a yearning as well as reluctance to get back to normalcy as soon as possible with abatement of the pandemic. Similarly, the phenomenal growth of online shopping has changed the ways in which products are promoted, stored, bought and delivered. These have given way to new business opportunities and have also led to the demise of many established ones. Integrated global supply chains are fraying at their ends to meet the supplies and demands from various parts of the world.

Driving all these is the relentless growth of the digital technologies. While this has brought in several advantages, it has also created many challenges. Navigating business in the digital world is the basic challenge faced by all companies and their managers.

With greater penetration of social media, people in all countries have become more aware of developments all over the world. As seen earlier, this has revolutionised the way people see and buy products and services. Brand loyalty based purely on premium image by multinational corporations (MNCs) is taking a beating with the emergence of "value for money" shift in consumer's minds. While more avenues for finance are available, pressures to control costs and offer robust profits to shareholders are proving to be great challenges in managing the finances of organisations.

Further, this has also brought in greater awareness among people on growing inequalities. It is an established fact that the rich, especially the very rich, have grown disproportionately rich and the poor, the bottom of the pyramid, have become poorer. Women empowerment as well as emerging groups like LGBT (lesbian, gay, bisexual and transgender) all need recognition and expect acceptance and opportunities available to others. Organisations cannot just stop at paying lip service to the concept of 'equal opportunity employer' but need to implement the same in letter and spirit.

In the current global political scenario, the so-called "superpowers" are flexing their muscles and are becoming more and more protective of their industries and territories. Emerging nations, having suffered suppression by them are also jostling for niche space more vigorously. A unipolar world that existed with the demise of Soviet Union is once again witnessing great rivalries between the two economic superpowers of USA and China. Both of them and Russia are vying to be the leader in the global context with financial, trade and military might and unbridled ambition for expanding their territories and spheres of influence. These conflicts have created great tension and flareup among them and other nations which have aligned with them all over the world. At the same time, threat of nuclear warfare by any indiscriminate ruler in any one of these countries hangs heavily in the air and the United Nations has been reduced to a mute spectator. These have led to authoritarian leaders in many countries and democratic values and freedom of thought and expression have been curtailed.

How true this has played out is being seen by the unexpected invasion of Ukraine by Russia, started in February 2022. This war has been dragging on till today causing much human misery and disturbing the whole world with prospects of massive hunger caused by sudden breakdown of supply chains. The comity of nations is getting fractured, and the threat of nuclear warfare appears real. As far as business and management fields are concerned, companies have gone back to drawing boards to rewrite their supply chain configurations even as they have just started implementing new supply chain strategies as a fallout of Covid 19. Once again, inequalities are rising and while new millionaires are springing up fast, millions of people are staring at abject poverty.

With the devastating blow delivered by Covid 19, governments have once again become the major economic engines in most of these nations. Giant technological corporations that dominate the digital world are fighting fiercely to protect their turfs as well as make inroads into others' domains. In the process, they are dictating the ways we, the people, live since our modern lives depend on them. Governments are finding it more and more difficult to rein them in due to their financial and market powers.

Most of the world is facing the reality of environmental degradation and the growing green movement to protect the globe for the present and future generations is gathering force.

All these have naturally affected all organisations' priorities, objectives, strategies etc.

Summing up, we can say that "business as usual" or old ways of doing things will not work anymore. New, innovative ways need to be found to meet these challenges constantly in this ever-changing scenario. However, I would like to emphasise that these basic, classic concepts and ideas still hold good, and we need to modify the ways we practise them. The basic purpose of these booklets is to expose the readers to all these classic concepts that have stood the test of time in a simple and concise manner so that they can start thinking and working out how to put them in practice in the current context.

A.S. Srinivasan   **October, 2022**

A.S. Srinivasan

A.S. Srinivasan holds a bachelor's degree in Mechanical Engineering (from the University of Madras), a Post Graduate Diploma in Plastics Engineering (D.I.I.T. from the Indian Institute of Technology, Bombay) and a Master's degree in Business Management (M.B.M. from the Asian Institute of Management, Manila, Philippines). He has participated in the Global Program for Management Development of the University of Michigan Business School.

Srinivasan has over 25 years of experience in industry and 15 years of experience in academics and consulting. His industry experience is primarily in the areas of Marketing and General Management in companies like TI Cycles, Aurofood, Pierce Leslie and Cutfast.

His last assignment was with Chennai Business School, a start up business school in Chennai, for over two years. As the first Dean of the school, he developed and implemented the curriculum for the post graduate program in management for the first batch. Prior to that, he was working with Institute for Financial Management and Research (IFMR), Chennai, for 8 years looking after the partnership with the Open University Business School (OUBS), UK in offering their Executive MBA in India. Apart from handling courses in the PGDM program of IFMR, he was actively involved in offering Management Development Programs (MDPs) to corporates and in consultancy assignments.

His current interests are in the areas of Management, Business, Economics etc. where he would like to keep himself updated with recent developments. He has taken to publishing blogs on these subjects for private circulation.

A.S. Srinivasan
A1/3/4, "Srinivas", Third Main Road,
Besant Nagar, Chennai 600 090
Mobile: 91 98414 01721
Email: sansrini@gmail.com

Printed in Great Britain
by Amazon

42530022R00046